# Hedgehugs

## Steve Wilson & Lucy Tapper

Henry Holt and Company
NEW YORK

Horace and Hattie are
the very best of friends.

There are so many things
they like to do together.

They like to search for

four-leaf clovers in the meadow.

They like to make daisy chains

in the shade of the old oak tree.

They like to splash

in puddles on the lawn.

And sometimes they like to
have a tea party by the river.

When Horace is busy,
Hattie puts on her tutu
and dances in the bluebells.

When Hattie is busy,
Horace searches for
spiders in the woods.

Horace and Hattie are
the very best of friends.

But there is one thing
they cannot do together.

They cannot hug.

They are just too spiky!

They have tried lots of ways to hug.

In the winter, they rolled in the snow until it covered all their quills.

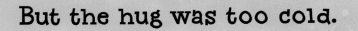

But the hug was too cold.

In the spring, they found some old, hollow logs.

Horace and Hattie squeezed inside.

But the hug was too bumpy.

In the summer, they stuck
strawberries on their spikes.

But the hug was too sticky.

In the autumn, they covered their
quills in crunchy, crispy leaves.

But the hug was too scratchy.

Poor Horace and Hattie.

Then one day, they found
something very interesting.

It was soft.

Was it a hat?

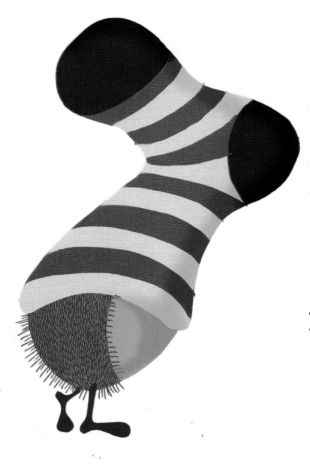

Horace decided to investigate.

He wriggled
and jiggled
and nibbled.

Then out he **popped!**

Hattie thought Horace
looked very funny.

Then she had
an idea.

Hattie looked at Horace.

Horace looked at Hattie.

They moved closer and **closer** and **closer** until . . .

. . . they hugged!

The hug was just right.

Not cold, not scratchy, not sticky, and not bumpy.

It was warm and soft and cuddly and comfy.

A perfect hedgehug!

So the next time you see someone wearing mismatched socks, or if one of your socks goes missing, you know what it means.

A **hedgehug** has happened!

For the Greats, the Grands, and the Girls

x

Henry Holt and Company, LLC
*Publishers since 1866*
175 Fifth Avenue, New York, New York 10010
mackids.com

Library of Congress Cataloging-in-Publication Data
Wilson, Steve, 1974—
Hedgehugs / Steve Wilson and Lucy Tapper. — First American edition.
   pages      cm
"First published in the United Kingdom in 2014 by Maverick Arts Publishing Ltd."—Copyright page.
Summary: "Horace and Hattie are hedgehogs, and the very best of friends. Together, they make
daisy chains, splash in puddles, and have tea parties. But there is one thing they can't do—hug!
They are just too spiky. Throughout the seasons, these two hedgehogs will try many different ways
of hugging. But will Horace and Hattie find a hug that feels just right?" —Provided by publisher.
ISBN 978-1-62779-404-6 (hardback)  •  ISBN 978-1-62779-413-8 (board book)
[1. Hedgehogs—Fiction. 2. Friendship—Fiction. 3. Hugging—Fiction.]
I. Tapper, Lucy, illustrator. II. Title.
PZ7.1.W58He  2015        [E]—dc23            2014048566

Henry Holt books may be purchased for business or promotional use. For information
on bulk purchases, please contact the Macmillan Corporate and Premium Sales
Department at (800) 221-7945 x5442 or by e-mail at specialmarkets@macmillan.com.

First published in the United Kingdom in 2014
by Maverick Arts Publishing Ltd.
First American edition—2015
Printed in China by RR Donnelley Asia Printing Solutions Ltd.,
Dongguan City, Guangdong Province

1  3  5  7  9  10  8  6  4  2